Gracie and her older brother, Freddie, are chasing each other inside their goldfish bowl, stirring up shells and shiny blue pebbles. Gracie, who never keeps still, feels dizzy and stops. She wants to whisper a secret to Freddie, but he flicks his slippery tail in her face and swims off.

She has to tell *somebody*, but who? "Nobody in my family understands," thinks Gracie. She stares through the glass at the fuzzy world beyond her bowl.

"I *know* I can tell someone out there."

Gracie swims to the top of the bowl. When her
family isn't looking, she smacks the water with her
fins to make tall waves, which rock higher and higher.

"Cut that out!" yells Gracie's father.

"Wow, that's cool," says Freddie.

Gracie keeps splashing. One of the waves pushes her up so
high, it spills her right over the top of the bowl. She falls onto a
thick carpet with a fat splat. She tries to swim away quickly but
her fins stick to the carpet, which feels nubbly and dry.

"Gotta go, gotta go, I'm a goldfish on the go."

But Gracie goes nowhere. She feels fingers around her stomach — a huge hand is scooping her into the air. A moment later, it drops her with a plunk into a toilet bowl, then closes the lid. Gracie can't see a thing.

The hand flushes. Gracie falls through pipes that bend and end who knows where.

She drops through darkness into smelly sewer water. Peeyoo.

Gracie lands on a long, bumpy tail. A giant goldfish? She sees a long snout with a sharp row of teeth turn towards her. Uh-oh. That's no goldfish.

"Heeeellllpppp!" screams Gracie.

"Quiet!" says a low voice.

"Wh-who are you?" asks Gracie.

"I'm Mopey," says a sad voice. "I grew
too big as a pet alligator, so my family
flushed me down the toilet." His tears
hit the water like the tinkle of crystal:
plink, plink, plink.

"I *know* you'll find a way out," says
Gracie. "If *I* can get out of my fishbowl,
I can help *you* get out of here." She
points to the wall, where a ladder leads
to an open manhole way up high.

"But that's too high!" cries Mopey.

"Just try it," says Gracie.

Mopey rushes to climb the ladder, but
slides back down with a loud splash.

"I can't," he says.

Mopey tries again. Nothing happens.

"It won't work," he says.

And it doesn't.

Gracie whispers her secret to Mopey. "I *know* you can do it," she says.

Mopey stops, closes his eyes, and takes long, slow breaths.
His body relaxes. All is still. After a few minutes,
he opens his eyes and takes a deep breath. He
looks up at the hole. With determination,
he grabs the bottom rung of the ladder
and slowly pulls himself up. He
doesn't slip. He doesn't
slide. The hole gets
closer and closer.

Mopey reaches the hole. He looks down at Gracie. He looks up at the sky. He lifts his snout through the hole until his teeth gleam in the sunshine.

"I did it!" he yells. He disappears through the hole and flicks his wavy tail to say good-bye.

"Yippee," cries Gracie.

But now she feels lonely. "I wanna go home." But which way is home?

"Gotta go, gotta go, I'm a goldfish on the go," says Gracie as she starts to swim away in a hurry.

Down through the open manhole comes a long, wrinkly nose — an elephant's trunk! It sucks up loads of water and catches Gracie in the middle, like a blob of milkshake stuck in a straw. Slurp. Gracie tries to swim faster and faster but goes nowhere.

"A-A-A-A-choo!" This noisy trunk spits her into a puddle.

"Sorry that I sucked y'all up, honey," says a thundering voice, "but I was so darn thirsty."

Gracie looks up from the puddle and sees an elephant beside her, raising her enormous foot to say hello. But the gigantic foot is stuck to a chain, which rattles against a metal bar hammered into the ground.

"The name's Eleanor, but y'all can call me Nellie."

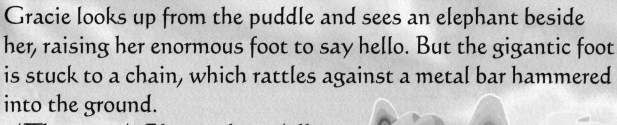

Nellie wears silver bells and pink slippers with a stretchy pink tutu strained across her belly.

"I'm sick of twirlin' on my tippy toes in the circus," says Nellie. "I wanna be free — but I can't be."

In a frenzy, Nellie pulls on her chain, but nothing happens.

"It won't work," she says. And it doesn't. Nellie tries again. Nothing happens.

Gracie whispers her secret to Nellie. "Just try it," she says. "I *know* you can do it."

Nellie stops, closes her big eyes, and takes long, slow breaths. Her body relaxes. All is still. After a few minutes, she opens her eyes and takes a deep breath. With calm firmness and confidence, Nellie pulls the chain with her humungous foot.

Snap. Another snap. Pieces of chain fly through the air. Broken bits of chain lie everywhere.

"I'm free!" says Nellie. "Thank y'all so much." She tickles Gracie with her trunk and they both giggle.

"I *knew* you could do it," says Gracie.

"Good-bye," says Nellie, who wriggles off her tutu as she walks away.

"Goodbye," says Gracie, who's in a hurry again, rushing through the puddle.

"Gotta go, gotta go, I'm a goldfish on the go — but which way do I go?"

Looking up at the sky, she muses: "I wish I could fly."

Gracie thinks some more. "Wait a minute, why not give it a try?"

Gracie flaps her fins, faster and faster, waiting to lift off like a bird.

"It won't work," she says.

And it doesn't.

"I can't," she says.

And she couldn't.

Gracie stops flapping and fussing. She takes long, slow breaths.

"I *know* I can do it," she says.

Gracie closes her eyes and lets the wind brush against her fins. Her body relaxes. All is still.

After a few minutes, Gracie opens her eyes and takes another deep breath. She flaps her fins slowly and gently. Gracie feels as if she's floating. Ahhhhhhhhh. She looks down and sees the puddle — it's now a tiny dot far below her.

Gracie is flying!

"Yippee, I'm free!" she cries from high in the sky.

Gracie swoops and soars over many houses. She flies down low through many backyards, until she sees her fishbowl through an open window.

She dives inside with a splash. Home at last.

"You're alive!" cries her mother. "I was so worried." She kisses Gracie and gives her a long hug with her fins. Gracie's father rushes to hold her. Even Freddie nuzzles up to his sister, placing his cheek next to hers.

"I missed you," says Freddie.

"We love you," says her mother.

"How did you get back?" asks her father.

"It's a secret," says Gracie.

She turns and winks at Freddie, who gives his sister his biggest smile ever.

For discussion:

Thoughts and feelings

What is Gracie's "secret"? (There are no right or wrong answers.)

Gracie, Mopey, and Nellie all faced challenges in this story. What thoughts and feelings do you have when you have a problem?

Have you ever looked at something that seemed impossible one day and then come up with a successful solution the next? What helped you to think of the solution?

What is confidence to you? How does it feel inside?

"A positive attitude can help you succeed." Do you agree or disagree? Why?

Can you think of a time when someone's encouragement helped you to succeed?

Behaviour

Why did Mopey stop, close his eyes, and take long, slow breaths before trying to climb the ladder?

Do you like to do things slowly? Why or why not? What happens if you do things too quickly?

What can happen when you push too hard to reach a goal? Think of an example of this in your life. What happened? How could you have approached the situation differently?

What do you think of when you hear the word(s) "stillness" or "calm inside"?

Suggestions

Self-confidence helps you to do things well. When do you feel confident?

Can you think of other things that you'd like to do well? Do you resist doing them? Why not give one of them a try?

When was the last time that someone encouraged you? How did it feel? When was the last time that you encouraged someone? How did that feel?

Can you give yourself five compliments right now? Think of what you have tried or done well lately, or how you have encouraged and supported someone else.

Try giving yourself at least two compliments every day. If you like, write them down. Consider your positive qualities, achievements, your dreams, new things you have tried, or ways that you have helped others. Pick the ones that feel best to you.

Remember: Everyone likes support and encouragement. Don't you?

CPSIA information can be obtained
at www.ICGtesting.com
Printed in the USA
251712LV00006B

9 780986 877605